Text copyright © 2015 by Jory John
Jacket art and interior illustrations copyright © 2015 by Bob Shea

Visit us on the Web! randomhousekids.com
Educators and librarians, for a variety of teaching tools, visit us at RHTeachersLibrarians.com

*Library of Congress Cataloging-in-Publication Data*
John, Jory.
I will chomp you! / by Jory John ; illustrated by Bob Shea. — First edition.
pages  cm.
Summary: A monster tries to chomp any reader who wants to go past
the first page of the book in order to keep his cakes safe.
ISBN 978-0-385-38986-0 (trade) — ISBN 978-0-385-38987-7 (lib. bdg.) — ISBN 978-0-385-38989-1 (ebook)
[1. Monsters—Fiction. 2. Books and reading—Fiction. 3. Cake—Fiction.] I. Shea, Bob, illustrator. II. Title.
PZ7.J62168Iaag 2015  [E]—dc23  2014026250

MANUFACTURED IN MALAYSIA
Book design by John Sazaklis
10 9 8 7 6 5 4 3 2 1
First Edition

To Alyssa
—J.J.

For Lorelei, Sylvie, and Athena
—B.S.

# I WILL CHOMP YOU!

**JORY JOHN**
wrote the words

**BOB SHEA**
drew the pictures

RANDOM HOUSE 🏠 NEW YORK

If you turn any more pages...

# HEY! I'm warning you!

You've been officially

WARNED!

Well, I missed.
But I won't miss again.

You do NOT want to turn
another page, buster.

You do NOT want these feet
running at you.

You do NOT want these teeth
chomping at you.

Oh, you're very good, buster.
Very good indeed.

Now I'm asking nicely.

Please put the book down.

Put the book down and read
something else.

Or go outside. Be a good kid.

Don't make me beg.

Okay, I BEG of you! Stop reading!
Please stop. . . .

# Sigh.

You're too good for this old guy.

I'm fast but you're faster.

I'll be okay. Just give me a moment.

You're probably wondering why
I'm so eager to chase you away.

Can you keep a secret?

*Sniff*

It's because I have all my cakes back here, at the end of the book.

See?
See all my beautiful frosted cakes. Cakes with sprinkles. Cakes with chocolate.

Cakes with strawberries and vanilla. Pineapple upside-down cake and pineapple right-side-up cake.

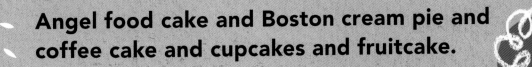

Angel food cake and Boston cream pie and coffee cake and cupcakes and fruitcake.

Yes. All my lovely, lovely cakes.

And you found them.

Most people don't get this far.

Most people are afraid of
all my chomping.

See, I don't like to share my cakes.

I want to chomp them all.

But ... I guess you can have a couple of these.

And maybe one of these.

And this.

Here you go...
just come a little closer...
a little bit closer now....

# Sigh.

You win.

How about this—
I'll give you half my cakes
if you promise never to
read this book again.

Do you promise?

You're not gonna start over,
are you, buster?

We're done, right?

Okay, I can see you're going to do whatever you want.

Fine.

Go ahead and turn all the pages again.

What do I care?

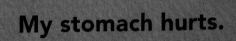

My stomach hurts.